I0712804

Turning Setbacks Into Comebacks

I

By

Brenda Lovett Arnold

In loving memory of my father, Phillip Dale Lovett.

Isaiah 40:31 states,

"But they that wait upon the Lord shall renew their strength; they shall mount up with wings as eagles; they shall run, and not be weary; and they shall walk, and not faint."

Grateful, thankful, and blessed have a deeper meaning than simple words. I can say I am thankful for supper and mean it. Being grateful, thankful, and blessed carries profound meaning. We must learn to appreciate the small things in life and never take anything for granted. Gratitude can also be compared to love. I love my dog, yet I really love my parents. Expression carries weight, though in different ways. I am so happy to have my dog. I lost my spouse five years ago to ALS. Today, I am thankful for my children and grandchildren, the bedroom I have at my daughter's house, my paid-off vehicle, the meals my daughter cooks, and my supportive friends and family.

I remember my dad attending my ballgames and my eighth-grade graduation. He has since passed away. My mom goes to many places with me. She is very kind and supportive. My mom also goes to all of my doctor's appointments.

Table of Contents

Blytheville High School

I taught at Blytheville High School from 2021–2023 before working at the high school, I commuted daily between Blytheville and Ocean to work at a private preschool. The round trip was two hours each day, and I put approximately 500 miles on my vehicle each week. My job involved evaluating children between birth and five years old. It was very fun to play with the babies, so I thought of it as a nice break from teaching at a public elementary, middle, or high school.

I don't remember exactly how I found out at the last minute before school started that there was a job opening for a high school resource teacher at Blytheville High School for the 2021–2022 school year. I called the Special Education Supervisor; she interviewed me and offered me a teaching contract. I was extremely excited, and received an $8,000 raise. I was hired for the resource position at Blytheville High School. I was completely honest during the interview.

I loved my job as a 9th–12th grade resource teacher. I taught Math, English, Science, and History. My students were a lot of fun, and I had a great time teaching them. I believe Blytheville High School is the most memorable school I've ever taught at, and it had the best teachers I've worked with.

First Workman's Compensation Injury before Ocean Elementary School

I fell out of the chair at the preschool where I was working, testing children for developmental delays. I knew I might need shoulder surgery. I was leaning over in my chair to hand a child a toy during the evaluation.

I was on workers' compensation due to hurting my left shoulder. It seems crazy and funny at the same time. It felt ridiculous that I could get hurt just by falling out of a chair. The workers' compensation adjuster sent me to a local doctor. Goodness!

He was the doctor that messed up my total hip replacement more than five years ago. One leg was longer than the other and it still hurt to walk. I rode the handicapped cart when I was in Walmart. I could not walk around the store or any store. My opinion of this doctor was that he should have been sued for messing up my hip, which still hurt in 2025. Also, after the hip replacement, I was told that I had a broken hip. I did not have a broken hip prior to surgery. I just shook my head; I wonder if my hip had been broken during the surgery.

The doctor was a young, dark-haired orthopedic whom workers' compensation required me to see. He recommended shoulder surgery. However, since he had done a poor job operating on my hip, I did not want him to operate on my shoulder. During the visit to his office, a workers' compensation nurse was in the room, too. I knew not to let him cut on me again, and I was entitled to request one change of doctor. I requested a change of physician.

The next appointment was with a different orthopedic doctor in Arkansas. This doctor had previously operated on my shoulder when my rotator cuff was torn. He was a friendly and tall doctor who appeared to care about his patients when they were covered by private insurance. He had a totally different approach when I was coming to see him as a workers' compensation patient.

I got hurt while standing next to my door in between classes. A student came running down the hallway, and the teacher next door told the student to stop running. The student kept running and never slowed down. I moved to the center of the hallway, telling him to stop. He grabbed my wrist and arm. My arm immediately began hurting, and I went to the office. The school sent me to the workers' compensation doctor immediately. Next, I was sent to the orthopedic who had operated on my shoulder for a torn rotator cuff. There were no issues with workers' compensation for this injury.

Although I knew the first orthopedic surgeon would have done surgery, I assumed the doctor who had repaired my rotator cuff would perform surgery again. I was so hurt hearing him tell me that he could not do anything for me. I had also learned at this point that

I did not have to let the workers' compensation nurse go into the appointment with me. I told her I did not want her in the doctor's office.

I do know this much: the doctor talked so loudly after I had the workers' compensation nurse leave the room that it was obvious he wanted her to hear everything he was saying. The nurse stood outside the door of the examining room, where my change-of-physician orthopedic and I were located. I cried hard and said,

"So you're just going to leave me handicapped? I can't even pick up my granddaughter. She's only one year old."

There was another day that I saw the student who tore my rotator cuff. He was running, and I yelled for him to stop. He raised both of his arms above his head and flipped me off. I could see his hand and his back as he continued to run out of the building.

Angel Junior High School

I knew that I couldn't wait until this school year ended, because I would be leaving Angel Junior High the following year. I was being transferred to Clark Public Schools and co-taught English 8, English 9, and Algebra I. I also taught a resource Math and English class. My son, Jimmy Roberson, attended Clark West Junior High in the seventh grade. I liked Clark West Junior High, and the school was located in a nicer part of town.

The school atmosphere was much better. There were places where students could sit outside, and the structure was not locked down after school. At the previous junior high, the building was surrounded by metal cages and gates. Once the bell rang for dismissal, everyone rushed out so they wouldn't get locked inside. This was not a friendly-looking atmosphere.

While at Blytheville High School, I made a goal that year to become more involved in the school's extracurricular activities. I planned to attend the ball games and social functions held at the school. My best friend Stephanie and I at an Ole Miss game, who is also a special education teacher, attended several ball games with me as well. We went to a football game in Trumann, Arkansas. I went to basketball games close to where I lived. The school was an hour from where I lived, but the away games were great, because they were easier for me to get to. I really liked basketball and attended several basketball games.

Rashaud Marshall

Rashaud Marshall graduated from Blytheville High School. He was the number one draft choice in the state of Arkansas. Wearing jersey #25, Rashaud Marshall signed with the Ole Miss Rebels during his freshman year of college. In his second year of college, he transferred to Arkansas State University, where he wore jersey #0. For the 2025–2026 school year, he signed with Austin Peay State University in Tennessee. I am excited to see what he will bring to the team during the 2025–2026 season at Austin Peay State University.

The following photos, taken at Ole Miss and Arkansas State University by Brenda Lovett Arnold, are included with Rashaud Marshall's permission to feature his images and story.

Rashaud Marshall at Ole Miss (2023-2024)

Rashaud Marshall #25 at Ole Miss

Rashaud Marshall and Brenda Lovett Arnold

Ole Miss 80 0.0 77
PLEASE STAY OFF
OF THE COURT
WIN WIN

Arkansas State University

(2024-2025)

Red Wolves

Rashaud Marshall at Arkansas State University

Stephanie and I at an Ole Miss game. Stephanie and I have been best friends on a personal and business level. We get along very well. I am so excited about the thought of us traveling together. We plan on traveling some this year if possible. We have taken trips together in the past. We took a trip to Oklahoma, Branson, Gatlinburg, and college basketball games at Ole Miss and Arkansas State University. I know we will travel to Austin Peay University this year to watch a college basketball game. Stephanie and I were in graduate school together. We are retired special education teachers.

Ocean High School

I taught self-contained at Ocean High School. The first year which was the 2023-2024 school years I only worked about one month. Then during the 2024-2025 school year I returned to work in September, 2024, because the IME doctor, Buffet, released me to return to work. My boss put me in a Kindergarten general education classroom.

Law Firm in Jonesboro, Arkansas

I had an attorney for one and a half years. He told me over the phone that he could not be my attorney anymore, since he did not have time to work on my workers' compensation case. He was behind since he had missed two months of work. My attorney then filed a motion with the court to withdraw as my counsel. I knew that once his motion was filed and he was no longer my attorney, the Workers' Compensation Commission would file a motion to dismiss my case. The urgency to find a new attorney was imperative.

I got Patricia's phone number from my old phone. Patricia lives near West Memphis, Arkansas. She is very kind and has long, dark hair. She has been my friend for several years. I first called her friend, an attorney, Mr. James. He told me that he could not take my case. I prayed; she was praying too. My friend, Patricia, gave me several leads for attorneys. The first attorney I called was based in

Jonesboro, Arkansas. The attorney's office said that I have two workers' compensation cases and asked if I ever go to Jonesboro. I told them that I actually go to Jonesboro quite regularly. I know this is God working on my behalf. I have an appointment with the attorney tomorrow! I am so happy! The woman I spoke with from Jonesboro wants to meet with me tomorrow, April 29, 2025, at 1:00 p.m. I am thankful that she wants to meet with me. I am extremely excited!

The Injury

The classroom closet should only have file cabinets in it. However, the file cabinet room had not been cleaned by the previous teacher, Ms. Branford. She told me she would return to clean out the classroom closet before school started, but she never did.

On August 30, 2023, I went into the closet to store a poster board and large sheets of white paper. Unfortunately, I fell and hurt my neck, back, and hip.

Mrs. Hall met me at the hospital when I was ready to leave. The Emergency Room doctor who treated me placed a brace on my right leg. I had a total hip replacement on my right hip several years ago. My right leg was placed in a brace covering my entire leg. Ms. Branford, had left the closet cluttered with boxes, personal belongings, students' work, and books. This made it impossible to access the filing cabinets. The special education director had also instructed Ms. Branford to clean up her belongings, but she did not.

In my opinion, I should not have been fired from my job, although a new paralegal told me that the termination was legal. I believe I was fired after I reported my injury.

The initial fall, when I hurt my neck, back, and hip on August 30, 2023, has long passed. However, I later sustained a second injury to my neck and back. I was taking a kindergarten student to the restroom. I was sitting on my walker changing his pull-up when he held onto my neck to steady himself. He put all his weight on my neck, hanging onto me in a way that I could not remove him.

I yelled several times for the substitute to help before she finally heard me and helped lift him off. I went to the ER the following day and learned that I had reinjured myself.

Over the phone, I was told that my second injury at Ocean Public Schools was not covered by workers' compensation. During a phone call with the Workers' Compensation Commission, where I can get free legal advice as long as I do not have an attorney, I was told to report the new injury and that it was indeed a new injury. This was my second injury at Ocean Public Schools.

I also did not receive the sign-on bonus that I should have received for the 2024–2025 school year. I believe this firing could have been retaliation from the Special Education Director. She was upset with me because she had gotten into trouble with the state department. She met with me when I was released to go back to work by Dr. Buffet, whom I suspect was influenced to clear me for work.

I was told upon returning to work not to call parents by the Special Education Director. This was a strange request, since we are normally encouraged to make positive parent contacts. A parent called me about a situation with her child, and I explained her rights over the phone. I did nothing wrong and actually did this to help my parents. I asked the state department a question to clarify the matter raised by the parent, so I could provide accurate information. I do not feel that I did anything wrong at all. I did the school a favor and especially helped the parent of the child. I am to advocate for my students and make sure all special education laws are followed.

I was terminated from my job at Ocean Public Schools while I should have been on workers' compensation. The workers' compensation adjuster said I was not covered. I reported the injury and was never contacted by a workers' compensation adjuster. This may have been because Mr. Rene filed a motion to withdraw as counsel, leaving the workers' compensation adjuster unable to speak with me directly. I still do not know why I was never contacted.

Court Hearing for Independent Medical Evaluation.

My mom and I went to the courthouse in Jonesboro, Arkansas. My attorney was there to meet me outside the courtroom. This was the first time I had met my attorney, Mr. Rene. He was well-dressed and courteous.

Mr. Rene, the school's attorney, the court reporter, judge, my mom, and I were in the courtroom. I felt nervous in the courtroom and had to turn my chair around to look at the school's attorney, because my head could not turn all the way to the right or left. I could not raise my neck up either.

I was sworn in, and the hearing began. The court reporter sat to my right, close to the judge in the front of the room. I sat with Mr. Rene on the right side of the courtroom. The school attorney sat on the left side of the room. I was not asked to go to the witness stand. The school attorney stayed in her seat, and we did too. I am glad I will have an income now. I have not had a check since December 2024.

The courtroom was large and uncomfortable. The school's attorney asked me several questions. My attorney sat there and never said a word. The school attorney won the case, and I was ordered to undergo an Independent Medical Evaluation.

Mr. Buffet eventually completed the Independent Medical Evaluation and was biased in his assessment. He never looked at my back, even though he stated in my medical records that he did. He even said my neck and back were fine. Dr. Adamentz, Tappen, and Mr. Bradford knew that my back was not fine. Otherwise, I would not have received injections in my back.

Even though the pain management doctor was giving me nerve blocks, Adamentz sent me to physical therapy. Tappen gave me a shot in the lumbar spine. Mr. Bradford took me off work. I believe it was due to my balance and my inability to walk well. The second time I saw Mr. Bradford, he had a totally different attitude. He sent me back to work with restrictions. He stated, "We will let the other doctors deal with you."

I am taking Dr. Adamentz's medical records to my new attorney today. This took place in July of last year. We had the Independent Medical Evaluation hearing at that time. We lost the hearing, and my attorney, who later withdrew as counsel, did absolutely nothing to defend me during the workers' compensation hearing.

A video was taken of me which contained several false statements. My attorney accepted the recording and did not object to anything in the video. The private investigator said that I cleaned the yard and walked in and out of the house several times. In reality, my mom and my friend Jim came to clean up the yard and fill in holes that my dog had dug. I am unable to do such work.

The investigator also had the nerve to follow me to Walmart. In the report, the woman who wrote the narrative about the recording stated that she could not record me in Walmart. She did not record me in Walmart, because I ride the handicapped cart. I was really angry about the recording and about my attorney, who didn't even bring any medical records from my neurosurgeon. Meanwhile, the workers' compensation attorney had medical records with her. It was ridiculous.

Mr. Rene told me several months ago that he was going to file for a hearing to dispute the IME report that Dr. Buffett wrote, which stated that I had no restrictions and could return to work. I returned to work in September 2024. I was reinjured on October 15, 2024.

The neurosurgeon that I saw in 2023–2024 practiced in Little Rock, Arkansas. He had taken me off work until further notice. Workers' Compensation made an appointment for me to go to an Independent Medical Evaluation with Dr. Buffett. Mr. Rene, my attorney, told me, "Do not go to the appointment with Dr. Buffett." I did not go.

Workers' Compensation filed a motion with the court for a hearing to determine if I had to attend an Independent Medical Evaluation. My attorney did not bring one medical record, did not defend me at all during the hearing, and made no objections to the surveillance video that was used against me in court, even though it was based on speculation.

In truth, I am relieved that Mr. Rene dropped me as a client. I now have a new attorney, and we have already had a deposition. Dr. Buffett released me to work in September 2024 with no restrictions. I have the text messages that I sent to the principal telling her that I was injured October 15, 2024.

Pain

I injured my neck and back again on October 15, 2024. I used my school insurance to return to my neurosurgeon's office. He ordered a new MRI of my neck and performed a neck fusion at C4, C5, and C6.

I am currently going to pain management and Affinity Counseling. I have completed paperwork at Affinity Counseling. I go to the Paragould office on Wednesday or Thursday. I arrive at 8:00 a.m. and will be seen at 10:00 a.m. the same day. Afterwards, I will be placed on the schedule to be seen regularly. I have already filled out my paperwork. Once I complete my initial intake and session, they will put me on the schedule.

I experienced anaphylaxis and was admitted to our local hospital. I was very depressed and, upon discharge, was transferred to a mental health facility at a larger hospital. I was inpatient for seven days. I told the nurse at Community Hospital that I was having visual hallucinations. This stopped the day I was released. I feel that it was caused by the medication I had been receiving. At the Psychiatric Unit, two medicines were added. I feel great now and have been productive. I do not feel depressed at all anymore. My family doctor had already increased my Paxil from 40 mg to 60 mg. I was already on an antidepressant. I had several changes that were very depressing to me. I was on worker's compensation. I only wanted to work and do my job. However, I was in pain and could not drive that far, and the neurosurgeon had taken me off work.

I also take Zyprexa three times a day and Topamax, two pills twice daily, along with the other medications I have been prescribed. The pain management doctor has me on Flexeril and Oxycodone. I do not take these often, because I cannot drive if I use them.

 I had been going to pain management. The doctor causes pain and does not numb anything. I am receiving nerve blocks because of the injuries I sustained on August 30, 2023, and October 15, 2024. Since it is a worker's compensation injury, they should be covering my medical treatment.

I am currently seeing a pain interventionist in Piggott, Arkansas, and have not returned to the pain management doctor in "Jonesboro, Arkansas," because Dr. Peral causes pain during nerve blocks as he only numbs the outer layer of skin. The new doctor uses lidocaine to numb deeper tissue before giving the nerve block. My last visit to the pain interventionist was on August 8, 2025. Since I am scheduled for surgery, he did not administer nerve blocks at that appointment.

The pain interventionist in Piggott, Arkansas, ordered an MRI of my back. I had the MRI on July 12, 2025. I was glad, since I want to know what is causing my back pain. My back never hurt before the fall on August 30, 2023. I was grateful that I had never had back problems before. Now I have back, hip, knee, and neck pain. It is very frustrating. I can either get angry about the pain or accept it.

I am continuing with pain intervention in hopes of lessening the pain. I want to be able to hold my youngest grandson and babysit him. I want to drive without pain and walk on my own in a store without using a walker. I would love to take a shower without a shower chair.

I know there are people in worse shape than me, and I realize that life can change abruptly in a moment. It happened to me while I was teaching. I would never have thought I would be injured simply by putting a piece of poster board and large sheets of white paper into a file cabinet room, although there were many supplies and books stacked high in the room.

Mom received a text message today about my appointment with the pain interventionist on Monday, July 21, 2025. I had the MRI on Saturday. He must already have the results. I am scheduled for a nerve block at L3 and L4 now that I have Medicaid. On August 8, 2025, the pain interventionist did not give me any nerve blocks since I will be having back surgery.

Dr. Phillips Spine Specialist

I am riding home from Dr. Phillips' office. He is a nice, caring, and pleasant spine specialist in Little Rock, Arkansas. I did not like the results of my MRI today. I have stenosis, and the vertebrae at L4 and L5 have slid over each other. If we do surgery, it will be fusion surgery. The pain interventionist doctor wants to do a nerve block at L3–L4. Dr. Phillips is scheduling me for a steroid epidural injection. I have another appointment with Dr. Phillips on August 13, 2025. I am supposed to tell him if I want back surgery at my next appointment.

I will be going on August 13, 2025, to tell Dr. Phillips that I want back surgery. I do not like that I have two slipped vertebrae and that they are affecting my hip. He said this surgery will help my hip too. I would love to be able to walk unassisted without my walker.

I saw Dr. Phillips, and I am scheduled for back surgery on September 17, 2025.

Complex Cases

I need to pick up my MRI's at the imaging center in Jonesboro, Arkansas. The law firm Beal Attorney's office in Little Rock has my flash drive from Mr. Rene. Since they said they could not represent me, they are mailing the flash drive back to me. My attorney told me that if cases get complicated and require work on their part, they drop the client and move on to easy cases.

My workers' compensation case is complex. However, my case seems simple for my new attorney. I went to a local attorney in Jonesboro, Arkansas, on April 14, 2025. I met with the Beal Attorney's office in person. A kind gentleman talked to me. He does workers' compensation cases. However, there is a team that handles only workers' compensation cases. Beal's office contacted me to tell me that they could not represent me. I got very busy calling attorneys. It did not take long to secure a new attorney. A Jonesboro attorney was glad to take my two workers' compensation cases. I feel very blessed.

The flash drive was downloaded in Jonesboro, Arkansas, and sent to the Little Rock office. They failed to return my flash drive. It had to be mailed to me. I gladly handed my flash drive to my new attorney. I am blessed to have such an awesome paralegal and attorney. They are super at their jobs and answer all of my questions. They have their office an hour from where I reside. This is convenient for me, and Jonesboro, Arkansas, is where I attended college. I am very familiar with Jonesboro, Arkansas.

In order to help me with my stress, I have been saying the Serenity Prayer. This little prayer seems to help me in stressful times.

Pain Doctor

I do not like the pain doctor because he does not give any numbing medicine before the nerve blocks. He does not numb anything. I think this is just crazy. You tell him so, and he just does not care. I also need a refill on my pain medicine, especially today. I will be taking a pain pill before I get the shot today.

Jimmy and Disability

Jimmy is my dear son, age 27. He had recent back surgery and will be undergoing another one on July 3, 2025. He worked three jobs last year and is not able to work at this time. I feel that he will be approved for Social Security Disability eventually. He was denied the first time. I believe that if he gets an attorney, he will be approved the second or third time.

The questions the disability determination man asked and the things he said make me believe I am going to be approved. He mentioned that I tried to go back to work a couple of times and how I was before I had problems. He also wanted to know if I could stand 6 to

8 hours a day. I absolutely cannot stand very long at all. I have a handicapped tag, shower chair, and a walker.

Daily Life

I take medication such as Oxycodone, Meloxicam, and Flexeril for pain and muscle spasms. I bought a lock and lockbox to put my medication into. Unfortunately, I cannot read the numbers on the lock. Therefore, I cannot lock my medication. I take other medications as well. I have Alpha-Gal. I take several allergy medications. Alpha-Gal is a new diagnosis from my allergist. I just had an idea: I could use nail polish to color-code the lock. Alpha-Gal means that I am allergic to red meat. I am also not supposed to have dairy, according to my allergist.

My bedroom is between the kitchen and laundry room. If I am not outside, I am probably asleep in my bedroom. Shiyah, my dog, goes outside and sometimes sits on the chair. I bring her on the leash to the front porch with me. She gets lots of petting everyday.

My allergist is sending me to Nashville, Tennessee, to see a mast cell activation specialist. She said I had Alpha-Gal, which is caused by a tick bite. I cannot eat any red meat. I am allowed to eat fish, turkey, and chicken. She also told me that I could not have any dairy products. I am also diabetic. The news is heartbreaking.

Nashville Trip

I spoke with Stephanie's mother yesterday about coming to Nashville with Mom, Stephanie, and me. She appeared excited: "You mean I'm going on a vacation, and I get out of the house?" she said. That made me feel wonderful.

Everyone in the group seems excited. We are going to Nashville to see my new allergist. Mrs. Culley is sending me to see a new specialist. I really hope he will help me. I am excited about going to Nashville too! Unfortunately we had problems with our vehicles and were not able to make the trip to Nashville, Tennessee.

Workers Compensation Attorney Dropped Me

Lately, over the past two days, there has been strange, unexplained, or suspicious activity associated with my medicine box and medicine. I have opioids, nerve pills, muscle relaxers, pain pills, etc. medications that I need and absolutely do not need stolen.

First, I could not find my box of medicine. I looked everywhere in my bedroom. I searched the entire room. Beth, my daughter, searched as well.

Beth helps take care of me. She took care of me after my neck surgery and will be taking care of me after my back surgery. She is such a blessing! She already prepares meals for me. My surgery date is September 17, 2025.

I am bad at hiding my medicine in different places and not remembering where I placed the medicine. I did buy a lock and a box that has a place to put a lock on it. I bought them to lock my medication in, I should use the medicine box and my problem would be solved. The only reason I hide my medicine is because I have had medicine stolen in the past.

My Lost Phone

I lost my phone. It held documentation and all my songs. I have not given up on searching for the phone. I need what is on that phone. My sweet friend, Patricia, recommended three workers' compensation attorneys for me to try to contact. I am expecting calls from each attorney's office tomorrow.

I have not found my phone yet. I am still waiting on my flash drive that was mailed on Friday, April 25, 2025. They are mailing my case file back. I think I will already be gone before the mail runs in the morning.

I have an appointment with the pain management doctor in Jonesboro, Dr. Bee, and my attorney. I just had to ask my mom for gas money. I am grateful that she had $40.00, but I feel terrible for asking her. She said she gets her check in four days, so I feel blessed and grateful. It is tough to be broke all the time and not have any income. I wrote it down, and when my Social Security check comes in November 2025, I will pay her back.

I hope I did not lose my phone by putting the weed eater in my truck. Jim put it in the back of my truck, and I slammed the back of the truck. I think I laid my phone down on the truck so I could shut the back. I know my best friend Jim would have closed the truck.

Jim is about 50 years old. He has dark hair, he is trustworthy, and he's always there to help me with anything. I do not want to be helpless, and if it is something that I can do, then I do the task, of course.

Taking Care of the Yard.

Jimmy, my son, told me not to mow or weed eat at the half-acre I bought in St. Francis, Arkansas. I talked to my cousin, Gerald, on the phone. He understood that I wanted to help. He agreed that if I can only do it for five minutes, then at least I helped.

I know it would make me feel better that I tried, for one thing. I know in my heart that I cannot do all of the yard. I bet I can do the yard for five minutes. I showed up at my property without the charger and feel like I should give the weed eater back. I was disappointed in myself.

Jimmy Roberson is my son.

Karson Roberson is my grandson.

Gerald, my cousin, now lives in Arkansas, not Oklahoma. I borrowed the weed eater on August 5, 2025. I used it for about five minutes before my back began to hurt. I did the best I could and felt a sense of accomplishment in those few minutes of use. Gerald encourages me to do whatever I can and helps with the things I cannot.

Profile: Special Education Director

Special Education Director: Mrs. Hiney

She wears makeup, frequently changes her hairstyle, and dresses well in nice clothing and jewelry. She cares about students with special needs. However, if she gets upset with you, like she did with me, you will see a different and not-so-friendly personality.

When I returned to work, she spoke with me and told me not to call parents. She wanted me to feel sorry for the teacher who did not clean up her mess.

Ironically, the other teacher who did not clean up the classroom where I was assigned, the previous teacher had fallen the same exact day and broke her hip. Mrs. Hiney's comment to me was not said nicely: "Well, you will get a workers' comp settlement." I kept my mouth shut. My case was none of her business.

She also discussed my attendance. The neurosurgeon and the workers' compensation doctor took me off work for the rest of the 2023–2024 school year. The neurosurgeon took me off work because I would not be able to change a student in my classroom if the paraprofessional was out of the room. I was unable to walk very much, stand, bend down, and I was unsteady. I was, in my opinion, a liability to the school.

Profile: My First Workers' Compensation Attorney

First Workers' Compensation Attorney: Mr. Rene

The first time I actually saw Mr. Rene was right before a court hearing. We had communicated via email and phone calls. He was dressed in a blue suit. He was of average height and had a friendly demeanor.

During the hearing, he did not oppose anything in the false narrative of the private investigator's report. He did not object to any questions the school attorney was asking me, either. I was defeated in the hearing. Mr. Rene also failed to bring any medical records. Nevertheless, the school attorney won the case, and my attorney was useless.

The hearing was regarding whether I had to see the IME doctor for an Independent Medical Evaluation.

The IME doctor was Mr. Buffet, who lied throughout his observation and conversations with me during the visit. He looked at my neck, but did not say anything about the radiologist's report or what Dr. Adamentz had stated. He did not look at my back. However, he wrote in my medical records that he had examined my back and that I was released to work with no restrictions.

Mr. Rene told me several months ago that he was going to file for a hearing to dispute the IME report Dr. Buffet wrote, which stated I had no restrictions and could return to work. I returned to work in September 2024, but I was re-injured on October 15, 2024.

Mrs. Penny served as my paralegal while Mr. Rene represented me. I emailed her my doctor appointments, physical therapy appointments, neck surgery appointments and dates, as well as any questions I had during the time Mr. Rene represented me.

Eventually, Mrs. Penny stopped responding to my emails. I then began emailing both Mr. and Mrs. Rene, along with Mrs. Penny. Mr. Rene was dissatisfied with the outcome of the hearing. He told me we were going to a hearing to dispute the IME report prepared by Mr. Buffett. Despite numerous emails and phone calls, I received no response.

Mr. Rene had represented me for one and a half years. One day, he called me unexpectedly. He explained that he had been off work for two months and was very behind. He admitted that my case was complex and that he did not have the time to devote to it.

I felt sad, angry, surprised, and determined to find other legal counsel. However, I had difficulty finding a new attorney.

Testimony

Patricia told me that she has a friend in Little Rock who is an attorney. She asked me to call him in the morning. I don't think I have my case file either, so I need to call the Beal Attorney Office to ask if my flash drive is there. If my flash drive is not there, then I don't know where it is, but I am pretty positive I left it with the Beal Attorney's office since I trusted Beal. I will call Mr. James in the morning and tell him that my friend, Patricia Brossett, asked me to call him. I feel really good about him. I do not even have to think about calling the Workers' Compensation Commission. I would like to get an MRI of my back, though.

Beal decided that they could not represent me. I borrowed Jimmy's phone and called Mr. James' office. The person who answered the phone let me know that their office could not help me with my workers' compensation case. I felt rather sad. I was also texting Patricia, my friend, in between the phone calls. I asked her to pray, and I said a prayer right then too. Patricia listed more attorneys for me to call. I dialed the first number from her next text after Mr. James and Beal.

I wrote down both that number and the Jonesboro attorney's number Patricia had sent me. I am not nervous or feeling much of any emotion at this point except defeated. I prayed again and asked in Jesus's name for an attorney who would work for me. I called the number, and luckily they wanted to meet with me tomorrow! God is so good to me. I was so excited.

In the morning I will go to Dr. Bee, my pain management doctor, and then meet with the attorney or paralegal at the Jonesboro office at 1:00 p.m. The last words the lady spoke were, "I will get the paperwork ready for two cases!" My prayer had been answered. I had totally given my problem of not having an attorney to God. Mr. Rene, my previous attorney not representing me anymore, turned out to be a blessing. I am so thankful, grateful, and blessed!

Dr. Buffet released me from care for my back, but never looked at, felt, or examined it. I could make an appointment with Dr. Adamentz, a neurosurgeon at the Neurological Surgery Center in Little Rock, Arkansas. I researched and discovered that he has high reviews and honors. I want to see Dr. Adamentz about my back as well. Workers' compensation sent me for an IME. I have a question since Dr. Adamentz is my doctor. I want a disability rating from Dr. Adamentz and a maximum medical improvement rating for my neck from him.

I need to call around and get the medical records from these hospitals. I do not really know which ER I went to after the kindergarten boy hung on my neck while I was changing his pull-up while sitting on my walker. The school administration was horrible and no help whatsoever when I told them I needed to see a doctor.

I finally saw Dr. Adamentz after switching doctors. First, I saw Dr. Tappen, who is not even a doctor but a physician assistant. He actually said while looking at my MRI, "If this were your insurance, we would look at it more closely. But since you are workers' compensation and you're not dying, I am going to release you back to work.." Immediately, I requested a new doctor.

I asked to see Dr. Adamentz, a neurosurgeon in Little Rock, Arkansas. I chose him to be my doctor because he has many years of experience and excellent reviews. He took me off work for the rest of the 2023–2024 school year. The workers' compensation commission asked for a hearing to get an independent medical examination. They won, and I had to undergo an independent medical evaluation. In my opinion, Dr. Buffet was paid well for the negative review.

Neck Fusion

Neck fusion surgery was in November, 2024. I want to nod my head as if saying yes to people, but that makes my head hurt a lot. It is May, 2025, and I am learning to hold my head still and not nod, because that motion is painful. My head is far too heavy for my neck. I have quite a bit of spasms and an unsightly scar that will hopefully fade with time. The scar on my neck bothers me. I do not like it at all. I did not like the neck brace either.

Pain Management and Social Security Disability

I am going to pain management and was approved for disability on April 8, 2025. Mr. Rene is no longer my attorney as of April 23, 2025. He said he does not have time to work on my case. I do not want to go back to pain management though, because he hurts me and does not numb me before giving an injection. They have a pain management doctor where I live. The lady at the physical therapy place told me today that their pain intervention doctor numbs patients first before giving an injection.

My brother has a nice friend. Since my brother is his friend, John has been a tremendous help to me. The property I purchased has grass that needs mowing and possibly weed eating. I want to get some tires to decorate like yard art. John is mowing and weed eating and hopefully will also clear out the junk. It is a big job that John is doing. I'd like to have some before and after pictures of the land. I feel thankful, grateful, and blessed.

I feel like I'm good at writing too. My goal was to write for 15 minutes every day. Now I am carrying a notebook with me, and it is working out well.

The school district fired me while I should have been under workers compensation. The workers' compensation adjuster may have lied to Human Resources, or the Human Resources lady may have lied. Mr. Rene was trying to figure out if it was an aggravation of an existing claim or a new injury. He did not do anything to defend me. He was useless in everything.

Jonesboro, Arkansas

I went to the ER in Jonesboro. I remember now. I think it was St. Bernard, but it may have been NEA the second time I got hurt, which was on October 15 at about 2:30 p.m. I better make it a point to go pick up my medical records from the date that I was injured. I went to NEA in Jonesboro on October 16, 2024.

Emails

I cannot find my phone. I have to pray. I have so many things on that phone. One is all the songs and documentation that I have done. I sure do not want it to be gone forever. My phone always shows up, so losing my phone is nothing new. I made several discoveries today. I am using my old phone, and I am still logged in under my school email. I am not getting new emails. However, the emails that I have sent do change a few things. For instance, an email that I sent to Mrs. Hall on 10/16/2024 states,

"I got hurt yesterday. I thought I was ok, but I'm not. I will be there when I have a driver in order for me to fill out the form."

The subject in the email that I sent to Mrs. Hall is *Neck/Back*. I asked for a form to fill out for getting hurt, and I could not get one. Mrs. Hall even said,

"Are you wanting to be a workers comp?" I said, *"No."*

I love teaching. It was very obvious this year that they wanted to get rid of me, and what was strange was every time a boss talked to me about anything, they made me sign and date the paper.

Office with my Bosses

Once I was called to the office and Mrs. Hiney, Mrs. Hall, Mrs. Ball, and Mrs. Suzy had me sign a sheet of paper after our conversation. At the beginning of the school year, Mrs. Hiney met with me to talk. The first thing she mentioned was that I was not to call parents. I went over parents' rights with one of my parents last year over the phone. Our parents do have rights, and it is my job as a Special Education Teacher to explain those rights. She informed me that I would be floating at the Kindergarten center, Jr. High, and High School. I was at the High School for ½ day once and the rest of my time was at the Kindergarten Center. I have taught for 25 years. I have no experience in Kindergarten and very little experience in elementary. I love teaching high school. I kept a positive attitude and worked hard at the Kindergarten Center.

I had a parent that did not like what happened in a meeting. I am not going to discuss this any further due to confidentiality. Once I was called to the office, Mrs. Hiney, the Special Education Director, asked me, "Are you allergic to work?" I have Mast Cell Activation Syndrome, and now I have been diagnosed with Alpha Gal. I get anaphylaxis frequently. This can happen anytime and anywhere. I turned in an emergency plan last year. It states that if I administer an Epipen, to call 911 and contact my emergency contacts.

My Attorney Dropped My Case

This happened when I no longer had an attorney. Mr. Rene filed a motion with the courts to no longer represent me as his client. I called several attorneys, and my new attorney took my two cases. I am thrilled to have an attorney who is actually working for me and getting things accomplished.

I called Workers' Compensation to inquire about my attorney dropping me as a client. The gentleman on the other line told me that it was a new injury when the child was hanging on my neck and that I had to report it to Workers' Compensation. He also said that an adjuster would contact me. It has been several days now, and a workers' compensation adjuster has not contacted me. As of May 10, 2025, this remains unresolved. I have to call Workers' Compensation to report that I got hurt on October 15, 2024, at about 2:30 p.m. As of April 26, 2025, I am under pain management care.

Dr. Adamentz

I saw Dr. Adamentz on May 6, 2025. He said I was at MMI on my neck and that I had a nine percent impairment rating. He wrote a prescription for physical therapy for my back. I do not like going to pain management and will not be returning. The doctor that I see does not numb his patients before giving an injection. Dr. Adamentz, however, numbs his patients before an injection. We discussed the injections and pain management in depth at my last appointment.

This piece of paper says that I got hurt on Wednesday, October 16, 2024. I was terminated on November 11, 2024. I received a notice in the mail about being terminated at the board meeting on November 11, 2024. I could not attend the board meeting since I was at a doctor's appointment. I did send the superintendent an email asking for a different date, though.

Bonus

I was supposed to receive a bonus for signing my contract this school year. I did not get the bonus. Instead, I was fired while I was denied workers' compensation and I had a neurosurgeon saying that I was unable to work. This is a right-to-work state; yes, I can be terminated. I feel like the paraprofessional in Mrs. Rais' classroom had been told to provoke me. She was always trying to boss me around. I let her say whatever she wanted and went on doing my job.

I know she was trying to change the boys since the office people always act like I have a problem with changing the two boys. I do not have a problem changing these Kindergarten boys so I don't understand why the administration appears to want me to think I should not be changing them or they want me to dislike being made to change them. I think they want me to quit. My first attorney told me, "Whatever you do, don't quit."

My Life is Changed Forever

My neck is fused at C4, C5, and C6. This has permanently limited my neck motion. I always rode roller coasters, and the front row was my favorite. We went white water rafting a couple of years ago, and we had planned on going back to Gatlinburg, Tennessee, to go white water rafting again. Unfortunately, white water rafting is no longer in my future nor are roller coasters.

Reported the Injury

I reported the injury to my principal. I called Mrs. Hall to see if this was an aggravation of the existing injury or if I needed to fill out a new form. I was disciplined for missing work due to pain the following day and was eventually fired. I went to the emergency room on October 16, 2024.

I have the text messages I sent to the principal. It was quite obvious they did not want me at this school. Frankly, changing pull-ups was not my job though I did so without complaint. I feel that my Special Education Director is at fault for my injury, since she knew my balance was not good, she knew I was on a walker, and she knew I could not walk fast. One of the students would run away, even going out the door while I followed as quickly as I could. Luckily, adults coming into the building intervened, or the situation could have been dangerous.

Workers' Compensation had already approved surgery at C5–C6 and to pay for that surgery. This was not the surgery that Dr. Adamentz suggested. The doctor that Workers' Compensation appointed reviewed my medical records also agreed that surgery on C5–C6 was needed. I ended up in a hearing and was required to see Dr. Buffet for an Independent Medical Evaluation or IME. He released me to go to work with no restrictions at all. He said that I was fine and no surgery was necessary. He lied in my medical records. He said that my back was fine. Dr. Buffet never examined my back and did a poor job of explaining the MRI, especially since Dr. Adamentz had already explained the MRI findings to me. I trusted Dr. Adamentz and his professional opinion.

The pain management doctor in Jonesboro, Arkansas, Dr. Gera Samil, checked my back and hips.

I also reported that I was injured to my principal via text. I have screenshots of these texts, which will be used in a request for a hearing by my new attorney (August 12, 2025). So in reality, this was again a Workers' Compensation case. Although Dr. Buffet released me with no restrictions, according to the Workers' Compensation adjuster and although they claim I am not a Workers' Compensation employee. It is ironic that I have a Workers' Compensation case number.

I was hurt October 15, 2024. I was at work October 15, 2024. I was not paid for October 15, 2024 since they cleaned the office with bleach and the secretary refused to sign me in. I have a condition called Mast Cell Activation Syndrome that causes me to go into anaphylaxis and my body reacts to bleach. I need to talk to the school about the date, because they owe me for working October 15, 2024. I texted the principal. I know I did not work on the 17th. I have since confirmed that I did not work on October 16, 2024.

The school district fired me. I was legally a workers' compensation claimant, but I was told by the human resources lady, Mrs. Hall, that I was not eligible for workers' compensation. Dr. Buffet had released me with no restrictions.

I ask myself, What does that matter? I was injured, and my neck and back hurt badly.

Now my mom was with me when I saw Dr. Buffet. It was the most ridiculous doctor visit imaginable. He showed me the MRI and told me there was plenty of fluid in my neck. He did not include any statement about my back in his initial Independent Medical Evaluation or IME, and he never examined my back. Only in the new Independent Medical Evaluation or IME report was my back mentioned.

Mr. Rene kept saying that he was going to file for a hearing.
We went to a hearing in July 2024, to determine if I had to attend the IME or Independent Medical Evaluation, The reason Workers' Compensation wanted me to get an IME is because Dr. Adamentz, my neurosurgeon had me off work until further notice. Workers' Compensation wanted me to go back to work.

Rene did not object to the surveillance video or anything else that was presented.

Therefore, the work compensation attorney got her wish, and I had to go to the IME appointment. Personally, I feel like they paid him a lot of money.

Right before telling me nothing was wrong, Dr. Buffet said, "Now this is the part that you're not going to want to hear."

The only positive remark in the report was that I had high job satisfaction. I told him, "I love my job!"

I do love my job. I've had good times and bad times during my 25-year career, but overall it has been fun and full of special memories.

Phone

My phone is important to me.

It's becoming less of a problem, but what I really want are the songs and recordings of myself talking. All I can think at this point is that we will go to Cricket when we have $10.00, get me a new SIM card, and keep my same phone number.

One thing I can do now is get a government phone. Jimmy is out of minutes, and he can get a government phone too.

We need to go to housing tomorrow if they are open. We need a decent place to live. I need to call Social Security and make sure they have everything. I am also supposed to call Dr. Adamentz and the doctor at Vanderbilt to schedule with the allergist, Mrs. Culley wants me to see. I did all those things, but the trip to Vanderbilt was canceled because Mom's car broke down, and my truck needed a new battery which I now have but as of May 19, 2025, the check engine light is on. Stephanie is also putting her vehicle in the shop. I don't know why, but for some reason we're not supposed to go to Nashville right now.

Pain Management in Jonesboro, Arkansas

I had to go to pain management on May 14, 2025. I got refills on my nerve medicine on May 2, 2025, and it's probably time to refill everything again. Right now, the middle of my bottom left foot is tingling the most. I saw the pain management doctor on May 19, 2025. There's a problem with billing Medicaid since I have Ambetter they keep saying Ambetter is primary. The doctor wants to do a nerve block on the right side, but it won't happen unless I pay the $64 I already owe, plus another eighty-something, for a total of about $148. Honestly, it's very annoying.

I spoke to someone in that office and thought we had taken care of it. But when I went there today, I had to be assertive with the receptionist again about the Medicaid and Ambetter issue. I had already handled it last week with two phone calls. I moved my left foot and it was still tingling under my toes in the middle of my foot. The Cortisone shot I got in my hip helped for two or three days. The nerve block worked on the right side for less than a day. I have no complaints about the left side of my lower back. The left shoulder was in spasm, and my neck felt like it had a crick in it. This struck me as a little humorous. Sometimes it was better to laugh than to cry.

Local Attorney Office

I had a new law firm representing me. I called them twice last week, but with Monday being Memorial Day, I expected to hear from them on Tuesday. I wanted to know when my case would settle and how much my case was worth. Rene Law Firm stopped representing me as of April 23, 2025. It had been difficult to find an attorney to take my cases. I couldn't have been happier with my local attorney from Jonesboro, Arkansas.

Counseling and Hospital

Beth, my daughter, and I went to Paragould today. Dr. Pierce referred me to Arissa Counseling. I met my counselor. His name was Charlie, and I liked him. Charlie wanted me to see the nurse practitioner once and him twice a month. I wanted my family doctor to prescribe my medications though. I was afraid that she would take me off my medicine, and my medicines at the time seemed to be working. I suppose I wouldn't have opposed being taken off the one medication that was for short-term use only. I considered stopping taking the medicine and I was taking it two times a day most of the time. It was Zyprexa. I had been an inpatient for a short period of time after an anaphylaxis episode in the Piggott Community Hospital. I experienced visual hallucinations while in the hospital. I wondered if it had been because of the medication they gave me while I was in the hospital. I told the nurse, and they transferred me to the psychiatric unit at a different hospital. I had not been doing well in the new hospital and actually yelled at a worker. I do not have any idea what I said at first. Her response was, "You worry too much." That set me off. I started yelling and cursing, which is completely out of character for me.

The employees working on the unit escorted me to another unit. This unit housed people disconnected from reality. I would say that some of them had schizophrenia. I wasn't doing very well, and the unit I had just left had too many people for me at the moment. I stayed in this new unit for two days, and as I improved, they moved me back to the first unit where the stable patients were located. I eventually returned to the healthier unit and finished my stay in the psychiatric unit. I was released to go home when I had stopped rapid cycling. I am bipolar; however, I normally plan trips. I do not get angry with anyone. I knew I had been cycling, and it is not a good feeling. That's when moods shift several times a day. I would go from happy, sad, mad, laughing, for example, all day long. This does not mean it happened in that order or that those were the exact emotions, it's just an example.

Social Security

I was broke and had no idea when I would get a SSDI check. I was very happy that I was approved in three months for my Social Security Disability. If I needed to, I could get the attorney's office to write a letter stating that I had two open cases. I also needed to notify food stamps that I received a check from retirement.

Medication

I took my medicine with me to the doctor. I couldn't find it afterward. I hoped Beth would tell me in the morning it was in the truck. I would have been in trouble if it was lost. While at counseling, we talked a bit about my neck, first marriage, and my sister. We did not stay on any of the topics very long. When he wanted me to discuss my first marriage, I asked him if we had to go there, and he nicely said, "Yes."

I tried to remain calm about my medicine bag not being in plain sight. It would've helped a lot if I had found my glasses.

Since I had no income to pay my rent or bills. Beth took care of me and helped me with showers and getting dressed. I was deeply appreciative. She also fed me and was a great cook. I was on hold for two hours to talk to someone from Social Security. I want to know how much money I will receive each month. I also want to know when I will begin receiving checks. They are using April 2,

2025, as my date of disability. I feel like my date of disability should be way before April. I applied for Social Security Disability in January, 2025.

After Neck Surgery

The neck operation and lack of motion have made looking at people more difficult, as well as riding in the handicapped cart, and driving. While driving, I must check the mirrors more often, than before the neck surgery, and I now turn my whole body to the left and right to see if any vehicles are coming while I am driving.

It is painful to turn my neck for extended periods while speaking to someone or watching a movie. The best motion for me is keeping my neck straight. I retain the same mobility prior to the surgery. Therefore, I am grateful that I did not lose any mobility compared to before. I cannot raise my head up. I can look down and slightly to the right and left. I can turn about 40 degrees in either direction.

Physical Therapy on My Back

I had an excellent physical therapist evaluating me today. The therapist did an outstanding job. I went to physical therapy for the first time last week. Both of my hips and both sides of my back were sore afterward. I had physical therapy on my back again today. She wants me to do my exercises twice daily. I can really feel the back muscles when I do the exercises, especially in my lower back. She stated that it would help with the sciatica, too. I need to do my exercises, and I plan to start consistently. I know my physical therapy exercises will help me if I do them. I want to stop hurting and develop whatever muscles can reduce the pain.

Workers' Compensation paid for physical therapy when I was first injured from the fall on August 30, 2023. That physical therapy was less effective than the therapy I am currently receiving.

While I was at physical therapy last week for my back, I irritated my right total hip replacement. My hip popped after I got home from therapy. For the next few days, it seemed as if my hip was trying to go out of socket. It was painful every time my hip seemed as if it were slipping. This happened several times, even while I was using the walker. I completed physical therapy and I needed a return appointment. Since Dr. Adamentz was retiring.

I began seeing Dr. Joel Phillips in Little Rock. He looked at the MRI that the pain management doctor had ordered.

Dr. Phillips said he would fuse L4 and L5 and that it would also help me with my walking. It would be magnificent if I could walk without a walker.

My preop is September 9, 2025 and surgery is September 17, 2025.

Referral to an Orthopedic

I saw my family doctor on Monday, June 9, 2025. He made a referral to an orthopedic specialist at Jonesboro, Arkansas.

However, I owe a bill and cannot be seen without a payment arrangement.

I had to leave a voicemail with the basic information such as name, date of birth, and phone number. I explained that I was disabled and would not receive my first check until November for the month of October, and that I had not worked since October 15, 2024.

The Mission

Beth told me that she wanted to go to the mission this morning. I got ready fairly quickly. I had already decided I wanted one of the ladies to pray for me before I even got there. I recognized a lady who attended the church where I grew up as a child. Her name was Mrs. Kilbreth. I asked her nicely to pray for me. Mrs. Kilbreth prayed with me about the pain in my neck. I felt different today walking around the mission. They have clothes, books, shoes, drinking glasses, and other items donated. Today I felt a sense of feeling thankful for everything I had chosen. While I was sacking up my items, I shared with the volunteer that I felt thankful and grateful. I told her there was another word, but I couldn't remember it. I just kept saying, thankful, grateful, and. I heard Beth say, "blessed." Then I said, "Yes, thankful, grateful, and blessed."

I am going to donate clothes I no longer wear the next time I go to the mission. It is the best and the correct thing to do. I have been blessed with shoes, purses, dresses, skirts, shirts, and pants. I want to give back to the mission.

I did get pants today that were smaller than the size 18's I had worn for at least the past 10 years. I weighed myself last night. I am so happy with 237 pounds. I started at 259 pounds. I am now a size 16 instead of an 18. This is the largest I have ever been in my life. I have been depressed for a very long time. I would eat a lot or binge eat.

I was thrilled to see Jimmy and his family today. Karson is getting so big. I could only hold him for a few seconds. He always has the biggest smile! He helped make my day. It was a very beautiful day and the weather was perfect.

I know that I qualify for Social Security Disability. I have been so aggravated lately because it hurts to turn my head to look at someone speaking.

Summer

My plan for the summer is to get a pool pass so I can go swimming. I love to swim, and it will be a way to get exercise. I will be able to do exercises in the water that I am unable to do normally.

I am so ready to get a house on my land. I am curious about the buildings that people make into houses. I need to search and find out if the portable building place is legit. I stopped at a place near Jonesboro, Arkansas. They have a huge building that is already almost liveable. The one I like has a high payment each month. However, it would include the insurance on the building.

I am still looking at a residence. I am currently looking at recreational vehicles, log manufactured homes, and manufactured homes.

I spoke to my mom about the building, and she agreed to pay $100.00 down and keep praying about this home. I am looking at sheds made into a house. It will be brand new, and it will be cheaper than what some people pay in rent. The building comes with insulation and electricity. I would still be able to design the building to my liking.

A lot of work has already been done, which is a huge plus in my opinion. I will still be able to design the house! There are so many advertisements for buildings online. I just do not need them to be a scam. I think it would be best to speak to a seller in person. I think a lot of the money should be paid upon delivery. It just makes more sense. I am interested in campers also.

I will sell my camper if I have to in order to pay the $1,200. It will be paid off in five years. But I believe I can pay it off with my work comp settlement. I have not been told that I will get a settlement,

Workers' compensation is not accepting responsibility for the neck or back injury that led to fusion surgery at C4, C5, C6, L4, and L5, God is doing miracles in my life, and I need to purchase a home, mobile home, recreational vehicle, or manufactured home to put on my property.

I got up and went on my Facebook and there was Stephanie, and above a video she had posted was the word "Grateful." She mentioned being grateful for the day and the sunshine. I finally understood the words I had heard her say on her videos so many times: "Have a magnificent day, moment after moment after moment." I feel this is a wonderful way to express being grateful.

It was the word "moment" that seemed to ring in my heart with such power and emotion behind it. It also goes along with what I have often said: "Don't worry about the small stuff. What's the small stuff? Everything." Next, I take my hand and make a closed fist, then an open fist as if I am throwing a ball. I pretend to throw all the bad or stressful stuff away.

It is the small, wonderful moments to be grateful for. Each moment is worthy of appreciation. We want to focus on those positive moments. A moment is a time when we can feel joy and happiness. Today, I am grateful for this moment. I hear the birds chirping; I see my dog enjoying the sun. The weather is perfect; it is very peaceful.

One of my favorite verses is, "I can do all things through Christ who strengthens me" (Philippians 4:13). I also pray the Serenity Prayer sometimes: "God, grant me the serenity to accept the things I cannot change, the courage to change the things I can, and the wisdom to know the difference."

Local Jonesboro Law Firm

I received the flash drive from the attorney that chose not to take my case. I had left my flash drive with the secretary, who wanted to send my file from Mr. Rene to the Little Rock, Arkansas office. An attorney declined to represent me in my workers' compensation case and mailed my case file to my address. I took the flash drive to my new attorney.

A wonderful attorney in Jonesboro, Arkansas, is now representing me in both of my workers' compensation cases. I injured myself on August 30, 2023, and October 15, 2024.

Feeling Sad

I am feeling very down right now. I lost my phone and do not have any way for anyone to reach me. I have an appointment in Little Rock tomorrow to see Dr. Adamentz. I still have nerve pills, but it is time for a refill. I feel sad and hurt. I just need $10.00 to get a new SIM card so I can have my phone working again. Mom has to save her money for the trip to Nashville to see the new allergist that Mrs. Culley is sending me to see.

I visited Dr. Adamentz the week of May 8, 2025. He assigned a 9% disability rating for my neck and referred me to physical therapy for my back. Dr. Adamentz will be retiring soon. I finally received an MRI of my back, which is a relief. I need to call the Neurological

Surgery Center to schedule an appointment with a neurosurgeon who accepts Arkansas Medicaid. Dr. Adamentz referred me to physical therapy, and now that treatment is complete, it is time for a follow-up appointment. Also, I must request a copy of the new MRI performed on July 12, 2025.

Blessings

We have more blessings to talk about. The church brought food and gave us $100.00 for our household. My daughter bought laundry soap, dishwashing liquid, toilet paper, and groceries. Then on May 6, 2025, a sweet lady wrote a check for the remainder of the water bill. That check kept our electricity from being disconnected, since the electricity and water are on the same bill.

I saw my daughter-in-law, Devyn, today. She came to my daughter's house. We had a great visit. She took the boys to the Car Show parade this evening. It was fantastic seeing her and my grandsons.

Dr. Adamentz's secretary was very hateful after my last visit. She told me my workers' compensation case had ended in August. She said she knew about my case and brought up a letter on her computer. She said she knew all about my case. Recently, Dr. Adamentz retired. I called to see one of the other doctors in the clinic, but my request was denied, since I have an open workers' compensation case.

Dr. Phillips

Today I called my son's neurosurgeon office to try to get an appointment with his neurosurgeon, Dr. Phillips. The appointment with Dr. Phillips is this Friday, July 18, 2025. My son has an appointment on July 18 as well. Our appointments are 15 minutes apart. My appointment is at 11:15 a.m., and my son, Jimmy, has an appointment with Dr. Phillips at 11:30 a.m. I really do not know if this will help my work compensation case or not. I will pick up the MRI disc and the physical therapy notes from the Piggott Community Hospital tomorrow morning.

I was able to see Dr. Joel Phillips at the Arkansas Surgical Clinic. The pain interventionist ordered an MRI. My vertebrae at L4–L5 have slipped. This means that one vertebrae is in front of the other vertebrae. Dr. Phillips told me that if he fuses L4 and L5, my hip pain would stop. I see Dr. Phillips again on August 12, 2025, to tell him whether or not I want him to perform back surgery. He said that if the hip hurts a lot, he would recommend that I have the surgery. I am using a walker since my hip hurts so badly and my balance is poor. I almost fall quite often, and my right hip remains in pain. I want to walk again unassisted. I want to take a shower without using a shower chair. I plan on having the surgery at this time.

Food Stamps

I received a call from the food stamp office today. She told me that I would receive my food stamps tomorrow. I previously had an issue with the food stamp office in Little Rock, Arkansas. The lady called me today to tell me they had resolved the problem.

Workers' Compensation

Mrs. Hiney - Workers Compensation Adjuster

Mrs. Hiney is the workers' compensation adjuster for the Arkansas School Boards Association. I have an attorney; therefore, I am not allowed to speak directly with her. After the second injury on October 15, 2024, Mrs. Hiney told Mrs. Hall that I was not eligible for workers' compensation and that I had been released with no restrictions.

During the time I was off work on October 16, 2024, and October 17, 2024, I used my last two sick days. The following Tuesday, I had an appointment with Dr. Adamentz that had already been scheduled. He ordered an MRI of my cervical spine. I underwent cervical fusion surgery soon after the MRI. Dr. Adamentz fused C4, C5, and C6.

The principal is Mrs. Stile. She is a heavy set blonde headed lady with short hair. She dresses in blue jeans and a nice shirt.

Family

Daughter – Beth

Beth is my beautiful 35-year-old daughter. She has dark hair and blue eyes. She is an intelligent mother and college student. She loves making TikToks and cooking. She also stays busy being a wife and mother to my two granddaughters.

Son – Jimmy

Jimmy is my handsome 27-year-old son with two sons. He has a pleasant personality. He is tall and has blonde hair and blue eyes. He enjoys gaming and cooking. He has two sons named Kyrin and Karson.

Stephanie, Mom, and Jim are loving and supportive.

Ocean Elementary School

While at the elementary school, the principal and special education director did not provide me with a laptop I needed to do my job. I was reprimanded one day for being in the computer lab working. I am not sure how they expected me to complete my work without providing the equipment necessary for paperwork and school email access.

After Dr. Buffett released me to go back to work in September 2024, Mrs. Hall, the special education director, wanted to meet with me in private.

She told me that I was professional. She told me she did not want me to call parents. She explained that the reason was because, the year before, a parent had called me with due process questions. I went over the parent's rights over the phone. The parent used those rights and took it to a due process meeting involving the state department. Mrs. Hall wanted me on a phone call at the meeting. Unfortunately, I was not mailed a Notice of Conference, and the state department said I was not allowed to attend the phone conference. I was actually at home, because Dr. Adamentz took me off work.

I needed the principal to know that I was having difficulty functioning physically in the classroom I shared with Mrs. Hall. At one point, I lost my balance and accidentally sat on a boy's hand. She was angry when I informed her the following day.

Later, I was called to the office, where Mrs. Stile, Mrs. Hall, and Mrs. Walker were all waiting to speak with me. The meeting felt more like an attack. Mrs. Walker asked me if I was "allergic to work." Mrs. Hall asked me if I wanted to be on workers' compensation after the second incident in which a boy hung on my neck, resulting in neck fusion surgery. It was quite obvious that they wanted to get rid of me.

Every time anyone spoke with me, I had to sign a document. This has never happened to me in my 25 years of teaching, and I have never had any write-ups.

The Law Changed

The Arkansas Department of Education had decided that special education teachers would be placed in general education classrooms rather than having their own resource classrooms. My placement for the 2023–2024 school term was in a kindergarten classroom. I was to spend the morning with one teacher and the afternoon with a different teacher. There were two autistic children in each of these kindergarten classrooms.

Great Teacher

There was a wonderful teacher and paraprofessional in one classroom. We worked very well together as a team. I worked with all of the students and also worked with the students specifically assigned to me, focusing on their IEP goals.

Teacher, Principal, and Paraprofessional

The other teacher and her paraprofessional treated me as if I was not welcome in the classroom, and they would rather the two autistic students had not been in their classroom. The special education paraprofessional quit, and there was a substitute paraprofessional who took her place. The special education paraprofessional works with the Special Education Teacher, and in my experience, the substitute has always worked with the Special Education Teacher.

The principal sent me a nasty email about having the Special Education Paraprofessional help me. I found this absolutely absurd. This was in Mrs. Rain's classroom. Her paraprofessional was a young adult who was extremely bossy and difficult to get along with. She told me one day as she passed me, "You were supposed to change the boys." I said, "I did change them." She did not say a word and kept walking. It almost felt like she was told to be hateful to me I really do not know. Once, she said changing their pull-ups was above her pay grade. On October 15, 2024 the date I was injured, I took the Special Education substitute with me while I changed pull-ups. I did this in case she ever had to change them. She needed to know where everything was located and what to expect.

The classroom paraprofessional who works with Mrs. Rain said, "I can change them." I politely said, "No, that is my job." She shut up and did not say another word. I could not change the students in the classroom restroom because the floor was extremely slick. Mrs. Stile said they had put epoxy on the floor in the bathrooms. I would take the students to the classroom next door that was not being used. I had to follow the special education minutes for how long the students were in the general education classroom. Prior to my working there, however, the paraprofessional would keep the boys next door in the empty room and let them play and watch cartoons.

I do not remember why I needed the paraprofessional one day from the other classroom. However, I did need her. I asked Mrs. Rain to go get her. She told me no. I was appalled really, I needed her and she would not go get her. I kept my thoughts to myself. Every day when she started sanitizing the room, I had to leave because I can go into anaphylaxis around cleaners.

I got into trouble on October 15, 2024, and received a formal reprimand. I had just gotten hurt from the student who was hanging on my neck. I planned on going into the building to report the injury.

As soon as I opened the door, the lady was mopping the floor with bleach. The only choice I had was to turn around and not go into the building. The reason I got into trouble was because I went and sat in my truck and left 15 minutes early. I did not remember that the clock in my truck was 15 minutes fast.

On a previous day, I walked into the office to sign in. The office had a strong bleach smell, and I began wheezing immediately. I sent the principal an email that I was going into anaphylaxis. She even griped at me for sending an email. The appropriate thing, according to her, was to sign out. How was I supposed to sign out? Perhaps she needs to go look up the definition of anaphylaxis.

I worked October 15, 2024 the day I got hurt and avoided the office due to the bleach smell. I contacted the secretary and asked her to sign me in on October 15, 2024. She told me she could not sign me in. I really do not know if I got paid for that day or not. I suppose I will never know.

I reported my injury to my principal when the boy was hanging on my neck. Mrs. Hall called me and said that Mrs. Hiney said I was not a workers' compensation case and that I was released to go to work with no restrictions. I told her I hurt my neck and back. I believe it was a different conversation when Mrs. Hall told me to talk to my attorney.

Mr. Rene said that it was an aggravation of an existing claim and I did not need to fill out a new workers' compensation form. I reported the new injury to Dr. Adamentz. I took myself to the hospital, and my family took me to my doctor's appointment in Little Rock to see Dr. Adamentz. I used my school insurance to see him. Dr. Adamentz performed neck surgery on November 17, 2024 on my C-spine. He fused cervical 4, cervical 5, and cervical 6.

Deposition

My attorney set up a meeting called a deposition. It included my attorney, the workers' compensation attorney, a court recorder, and me. During the deposition, she wanted to ask about previous injuries to my neck. An employer hires an employee "as is." I was active before August 30, 2023. I went to amusement parks. I love roller coasters. I had a blast white-water rafting. My friends and I love taking trips.

 Today, my deposition was at my attorney's office. My attorney told me not to talk too much. During a break, he said I had been talking too much. The school's attorney asked if I called my workers' compensation adjuster a liar. I know I did not say the word *liar*. I cannot remember if I said she lied or not.

Once the deposition was over, I realized that I had not told the school's attorney what allergy pills I take. I take so much medication that it is hard to list everyone of them in a short amount of time.

I did share that I sent my principal an email on October 15, 2024, asking the name of the special education substitute, and that Mrs. Hall never emailed me back. I also sent this in a text that I provided to my attorney in Jonesboro. They will have it for the upcoming hearing. The date for the upcoming hearing has not been set yet.

This child held onto my neck for more than a minute. The child weighed about 50 pounds. I took the special education substitute with me while I changed the student's pull-up. I am very grateful that I did, since the child hung onto my neck with all his weight while I sat on the seat of my walker.

I got in trouble for leaving 15 minutes early on the same date October 15, 2024, a date that the secretary would not even sign me in. I was hurt and sat in my truck until it was time to go. I began hurting immediately. I texted the principal after it happened. I had forgotten that the time in my truck was set fifteen minutes ahead.

I went to either St. Bernard's or NEA. After calling both hospitals, I confirmed that I went to NEA on October 16, 2024. I will have to pick up my medical records. Mrs. Hall made me sign a written reprimand about leaving early. I left and went straight to the emergency room I thought. I sent her an email apologizing and explaining that my truck's time was set fast. I waited until the following day to go to the Emergency room at NEA hospital.

I met my mom at her church today. It is Mother's Day. I asked for prayers this week. I have a lot that I am going through.

Jimmy, my son, gets an MRI on May 13 and will see the neurosurgeon in Little Rock on May 14, 2024. I am scheduled to see my family doctor. I will have to reschedule that appointment, since I must go to my attorney's office to meet with her, the school's attorney, and the court recorder.

I have been in touch with my paralegal in Jonesboro, Arkansas. She has told me that my attorney is requesting a hearing with the workers' compensation commission.

There is a pre-hearing first to set the date for the actual hearing. The hearing is being requested due to my last injury that happened on October 15, 2024.

Today, I am nervous about the deposition. I know the answers to anything the school's attorney or my attorney asks me.

I should never have gotten hurt. My job as a school teacher does not, and never has, involved changing pull-ups. Children with pull-ups have a one-on-one paraprofessional or a special education paraprofessional. I feel like calling the state department and asking if changing pull-ups is part of my job.

I have the workers' compensation meeting on May 15, 2025. I still do not fully understand what a deposition is, except that both attorneys will be asking me questions. During the deposition break, my attorney felt I was talking too much.

I think the answers to my deposition were fine. The ending, in particular, seemed to be what my attorney will base his case on. I never wanted to be a workers' compensation employee. I did not choose to get hurt on the job. I am a Special Education Teacher. I have been teaching for twenty-five years, and I had planned on teaching for at least ten more years.

My career made me happy to go to work. Teaching is a career that I put my heart and soul into, and I will always love my students. My students brought incredible meaning into my life, even if the students never knew it. They made me a better person. I am more patient, I know.

The attorney's office has stairs in the building, and the restroom is located upstairs. My main concern is whether or not I will have to walk up and down the stairs. I will also need to find something nice to wear. The thought of being put on the spot by the school's attorney is also daunting. I have already met her; last year she was present at the hearing about whether I had to go to the Independent Medical Evaluation with Dr. Buffet.

I know what to expect from the school attorney. She is not a nice person and can make me feel like I am on trial, as if I did something wrong. But I know I did not do anything wrong. There is one question that she asks that I wish she would not ask. She has asked me twice: "How did you break your neck?" My answer is: "I jumped out of a car while my first husband was beating me." She already knows this answer. Besides, it happened over 30 years ago.

I am thankful that my attorney was there during the deposition. I also like my paralegal—she is kind, calm, and helpful. I sent her an email this morning because I am concerned about a few of the things I said during the deposition. I left out a job that I had for two years. I forgot several of the medications that I take. I also did not list all of my diagnoses. I spoke about depression and anxiety in depth, and about my deceased husband, but I failed to mention Mast Cell Activation Syndrome, Alpha-Gal, and Bipolar Disorder.

I know she has all of my medical records, so I am not too concerned. What puzzled me was why she asked if I had called the workers' compensation adjuster a liar. I never said those exact words. I probably said that she lied. My second workers' compensation injury was not, according to them, a workers' compensation injury at all that's what I was told by Mrs. Hall in Human Resources.

She told me that Mrs. Hiney said I was released with no restrictions, and therefore this was not a workers' compensation matter. I was surprised when I called the workers' compensation commission to report the incident. I had to call the workers' compensation number, but I did fill out the form that the school refused to provide me.

Mrs. Kara, the attorney for the school, knows that I qualified for Social Security Disability in three months without an attorney. I told her I would receive my first check in November. That was truly a blessing, since most people are denied the first time and need an attorney. She knows I had surgery on my neck and re-injured myself on October 15, 2024, while changing a student's pull-up. I really wish this whole incident had never happened. I never thought I would get injured again. If I had looked into the future and had known that I was going to have neck surgery and be permanently disabled, I would've resigned when Dr. Buffet sent me back to work with no restrictions.

My bosses seemed determined to remind me that my job was to change pull-ups. I feel like they wanted me to quit or expected me to quit. They were negative toward me and seemed to single me out. This is how I felt, and I did not feel welcome at work. I have never worked at a school where the teachers tattled on one another. I have taught for 25 years, and I felt as if I worked alone without any help from anyone. The paraprofessional in Mrs. Dell's classroom acted as if her job was to give me a hard time, or as if she was told to give me a hard time. My bosses seemed to give me more work than was possible to complete. However, I worked hard and always completed the work every day. I was never accepted as a professional at this school and felt more unwelcome than anything else.

During the deposition, the school's attorney had the audacity to ask if I was ever going to work again. I simply answered, "No." Was she simply being obtuse? She already knew I qualified for Social Security Disability.

I am going to counseling for depression. The school attorney knows I am going to counseling as well, and I don't care. I am not happy that I cannot work, walk normally, that I stumble, must use a walker, rely on a shower chair and an elevated toilet seat, carry a handicapped tag, suffer pain in multiple body parts, and attend both physical therapy and pain management at the same time.

Hurting

I am sitting on the porch. My lower back is hurting, and it is tingling under my toes on my left foot. The second and third toes have some numbness compared with the rest of the toes on the left foot and the toes on the right foot. I took a pain pill and a muscle relaxer. I took Oxycodone and Flexeril. I should get on the schedule this week for physical therapy. I completed 10 sessions of physical therapy, and there was no improvement in my back. I went to Dr. Joel Phillips in Little Rock, Arkansas. My next appointment is August 13, 2025, to discuss whether or not I want to have a fusion at L4 and L5.

I am grateful the child did not break my neck. I am thankful that Dr. Adamentz was able to relieve the pinched nerves from my spinal cord and fuse the discs at C4, C5, and C6. I wish my back would stop hurting. I cannot settle my case until my back is all right. My pain level is a 7 in my lower back at the moment.

I have an appointment with a pain interventionist on Monday, May 19, 2025.

The lady responsible for billing wants me to call my insurance company since I have Medicaid now. Ambetter is my insurance provided through a grant from the state of Arkansas. Recently, I was also given Arkansas Medicaid, which required me to cancel Ambetter.

The pain interventionist does accept Arkansas Medicaid. During our phone conversation today, she shared that my bill for $46.00 is from the nerve blocks that I had received using Ambetter as my primary insurance. Right now my left pinkie is tingling, as is the toe next to the pinkie toe.

I changed my pain management doctor to a pain interventionist, because the pain management doctor does not give any numbing medicine before he gives you the shot. He only numbs the outside of the skin and does not give Lidocaine before giving the nerve block.

The work injuries have been detrimental to my quality of life. I use a walker to go any distance at all, even inside the house. I use the walker in order to walk to the handicapped cart at Walmart. I am not able to clean much. I can sit and stand, but not for very long. I cannot cook a full meal, because it hurts too badly to stand for extended periods. The neck surgery has limited how far I am able to turn my head to the right and left. I am unable to look up. Since I cannot look up, I am unable to see what aisle the bread, for example, is on at Walmart. It is frustrating, and I have to ask a stranger for help to read what aisle items are located. It all goes back to when I was injured on August 30, 2023. If the mess the previous teacher had been cleaned up, I would not be asking where items are located in Walmart and other stores. My local Harps store has a handicapped cart that has very little charge when I go shopping.

I generally try to avoid going shopping. My shopping trips are very limited. They consist of shopping for very few items. I am always with a family member when I go shopping.

Alpha-Gal and Mast Cell Activation Syndrome

I have not eaten anything that goes against the Alpha-Gal diet. My arms are red and burning. I am going to take two Benadryl. I am extremely thankful that I did not go into anaphylaxis. I definitely wish I could stop having allergic reactions. I also wish I knew what I am allergic to. The allergist told me that I have Mast Cell Activation Syndrome. This condition causes my body to attack itself. My triggers could be stress, temperature changes, and barometric pressure, just to name a few.

I was scheduled to see a new allergist at Vanderbilt in Nashville. My mom, Stephanie, my best friend, Mrs. Ellis (Stephanie's mother), and I had planned to go to Nashville and stay 3 nights and 4 days. Our motel reservation was for May 21, 2025–May 24, 2025. I was thrilled at the idea of going downtown in Nashville, Tennessee.

I had hoped to take pictures of the Grand Ole Opry and other tourist attractions. Unfortunately, we were unable to go to Nashville, and I had to cancel the appointment with the new allergist. My vehicle needed a new battery, Stephanie's vehicle was in the shop, and my mom's vehicle also needed repairs.

I am grateful, thankful, and blessed that my sweet mom managed to purchase a new battery for my vehicle today. The new battery will allow me to go to the grocery store and church in the morning.

I think my mom attends a good church every Sunday. I go to my church, Solid Rock, in Kennett, Missouri, when I have the gas money. I am blessed that I can go to my church in the morning. I am grateful for my new battery. This allowed me to attend church today. I am very fortunate to have had the chance to spend the day with my big sister, Sheri.

Disability

I just opened a letter from the Social Security Administration. I am teary-eyed at the moment. I feel sad facing the reality that they consider me disabled to the point where I cannot work. This is what my family has been telling me for a long time, even before I actually applied for disability. I know I cannot work this school year. I also know in my heart that I may be able to substitute half-days in the future. Many people get checks. I agree that I cannot work right now. I am going to be alright.

I never knew I would feel so sad upon receiving my award letter. Chris, from the Social Security Administration, had already explained that I was approved for disability. Still, seeing the letter in black and white makes me sad and teary-eyed.

I never wanted to become disabled or qualify for Social Security Disability. I only wanted to teach my students. I am crying now, and I know it is fine to feel my feelings. The loss of my career has been difficult for me. I know I am a good teacher. I am confident that I helped many kids throughout my 25 years. However, that does not change how I feel right now. The realization is setting in, but I won't get a check until November, 2025 and that is several months away.

Dreaming of a Home

I gave up my residence on November 1, 2024, as I was about to be terminated from my teaching job. The last injury I incurred led Dr. Adamentz to order a new MRI of my neck, after which he recommended a neck fusion. Dr. Adamentz immediately removed me from work duties.

I knew that I had used all of my sick and personal days by October 17, 2024, and that I would receive only one more paycheck. There was no way I could pay my rent or my bills without income. My daughter, Beth, graciously offered me a place in her home with her family. I now live with her, but also stay in my camper from time to time. I stay in my pop-up camper when it is not too hot since it has no electricity. It is fun, and I think of it as camping. I have a one-burner, propane-operated stove for cooking, as well as lights and a Bluetooth speaker for music.

I know that eventually I will receive a workers' compensation settlement. I have been looking at log homes, manufactured homes, and bumper-pull campers. My favorite place for the largest selection is Camping World.

This happened 10/15/2024

I got hurt changing a student's pull-up. He stood in front of me while I sat on my walker. He put his arms around my neck with all of his weight and hung on my neck. My neck hurt immediately. He would not get off my neck. I had brought the special education substitute with me into the room. I always change the student in the classroom next to his actual classroom. There is epoxy on the floor in the restroom in his classroom. The epoxy is very slick, and I do not want to fall.

I yelled loudly for the special education substitute who had been hired for the day. She did not hear me at first, but eventually she did and got the child off my neck. I am grateful I took her with me to the other room, because otherwise I would have been by myself.

Honestly, it is not my job to take students to the restroom. I have no idea why my special education director made me change pull-ups in the first place. She was not nice to me when I came back to work. In fact, she was openly hostile. I really think that she put me in a Kindergarten classroom because I have taught high school the majority of my career. Elementary is my least favorite. I am happier with junior high and high school teaching positions.

I sent my principal a text saying that I had been hurt. I told her that I would not be at work on October 16, 2024, and October 17, 2024, because of my neck injury caused by the student. I saw Dr. Adamentz on October 22, 2024. He did a new MRI of my neck and scheduled me for neck fusion of Cervical 4, Cervical 5, and Cervical 6.

I am going to pain management for my back in Jonesboro with Dr. Gera Samu. I have had a Cortisone shot in my hip and three injections in both sides of my back. My next appointment is to determine if the shots helped me at all, and to develop a plan of action. At the following appointment, he plans to perform a nerve block on the right side to evaluate whether it provides relief from my back pain.

Patricia and her attorney friends

I do not know why I am so nervous about calling the attorney Patricia is friends with. I called and the gentleman took a message. I asked Patricia to pray and thank God for the new attorney. I need to slow down, stop now and pray. I feel so much better when I pray.

Social Security Disability

I received a letter today saying I had been approved for disability from both Darrell and myself. So I will be receiving a widow's benefit, too. I would rather have Darrell back than get a disability because of him. I really miss him a great deal.

Calling Workers Compensation Commission

Do I call the Workers' Compensation Commission now or wait for a call from the attorney? I already know the Workers' Compensation adjuster is going to work quickly to close my case now that Mr. Rene, my attorney, has filed to no longer represent me. I absolutely do not want my case closed.

I have to locate the flash drive that Mr. Rene sent to me. I gave it to an attorney's office to send to their Little Rock, Arkansas, office. I remember leaving the flash drive at the attorney's office in Jonesboro, Arkansas. My nerves are not very good right now, and I am under a lot of stress. God is in control and will never put on me more than I can handle.

Going to Mom's

I am going to Mom's at 1:00 p.m., and I also have a prescription to pick up. My Shiyah girl is outside with me, sitting in the sun. She even knows that we need sun!

Special Thank You

Shirley Davis

Jimmy Roberson

Beth Tucker

Sheri Reeves

Billy Lovett

Brother Zack Parr

Stephanie Ellis

Gerald Harmon

Jim Fuwell

Rashaud Marshall

Big John Johnson